DAMIAN HARVEY was born in Blackpool. As a teenager,
he wanted to be a radio presenter so he studied
Communication Studies at Sunderland University. It was
while he was a student that he started writing stories.
Damian lives with his family in Blackpool. This is his
first book for Frances Lincoln.

KORKY PAUL was born in Zimbabwe and is one of seven children.
He studied Fine Art at Durban Art School in South Africa and
Film Animation at CalArts in California. His picture book series,
Winnie the Witch, won the Children's Book Award. Known only
to himself as the 'World's Greatest Portrait Painter and Dinosaur
Drawer', Korky regularly holds drawing workshops at libraries
and schools to encourage children to share his passion for drawing.
He lives with his family in Oxford. This is his first book
for Frances Lincoln.

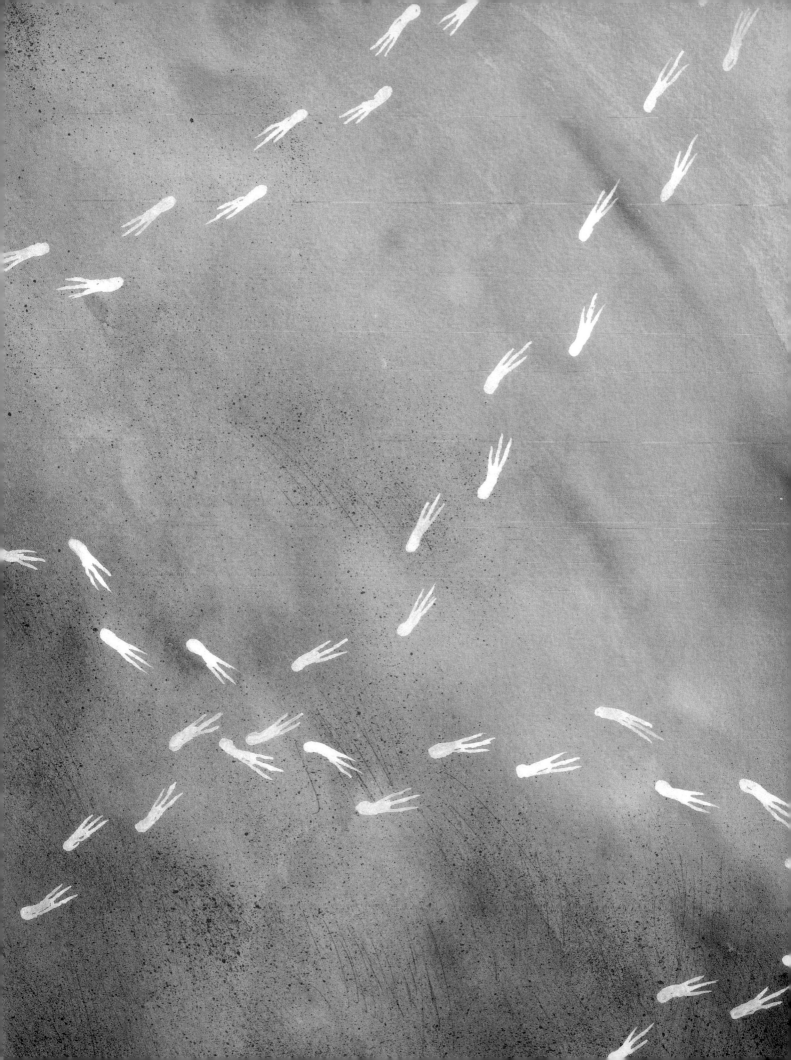

For my wife, Lorraine, with all my love – D.H.

For Mila – K.P.

First published in Great Britain in 2006 and in the USA in 2007
by Frances Lincoln Children's Books, 4 Torriano Mews,
Torriano Avenue, London NW5 2RZ

www.franceslincoln.com
www.damianharvey.com

Distributed in the USA by Publishers Group West

British Library Cataloguing in Publication Data available on request

ISBN 978-1-84507-642-9

Printed in Singapore

1 3 5 7 9 8 6 4 2

Snail's Legs

Damian Harvey

Illustrated by Korky Paul

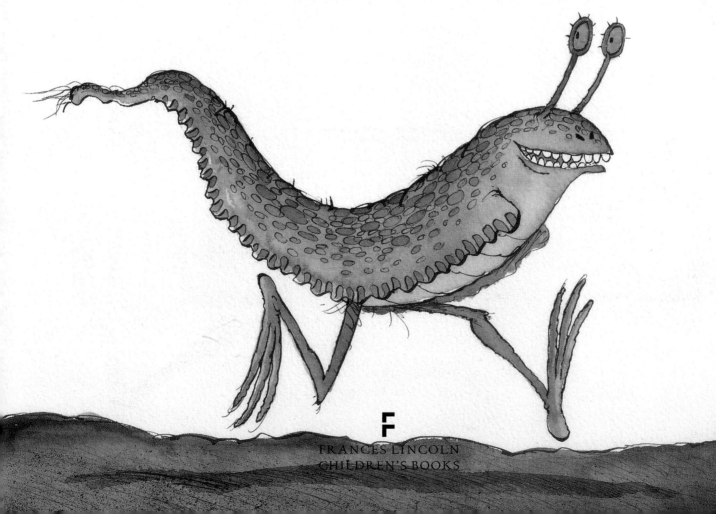

F

FRANCES LINCOLN
CHILDREN'S BOOKS

Snail

was the fastest runner in the whole wood.

Frog

had been the fastest runner in his younger days
but he was getting old.

Frog still came to watch the races
and he would tease Snail, saying
that if he wanted to, he could still
beat him in a race. Snail loved his
old friend and didn't mind
being teased.

One day Snail and Frog were sitting on a big rock talking about races they had won when they met a man walking along the road.

"I am the King's chef," the man said, "and I am looking for an animal with very strong legs to help me prepare a special birthday treat for him. You are both such fast runners, you must have very strong legs indeed!"

The two friends were amazed. They had never met the King and now here was a chance to do something special for his birthday.

That would be a great honour indeed.

Frog puffed out his chest and replied,
"Oh yes, our legs are very strong.
But of course, mine are strongest
as I am much faster than Snail."

Snail smiled at his old friend.
After all, everybody in the wood knew
that Snail was the fastest runner.

"My old friend here is a fast runner,"
said Snail. "But as you can see, he
is very old and I am the fastest now."

"Nonsense," cried Frog.
"You will never be as fast as me."

"My dear friend," said Snail,
"you do not even race any more."

Frog knew this was true, but he could only think how grand it would be to meet the King.

"I let you win those races," Frog shouted. "A puny snail like you could never beat a grand frog like me."

Snail was furious. "Right, that does it. If you think you are fastest, we'll race right now!"

Snail jumped down from the rock and put on his running hat.

What had Frog done? He could not
beat Snail. He was much too old to race.
He would have to admit that Snail was
the fastest and had the strongest legs.

But that would mean Frog would not get to see the King.
There was only one thing he could do. He would have to race.

The runners agreed to race along the road, through the wood, over the bridge and round the pond.

The chef held up his handkerchief.

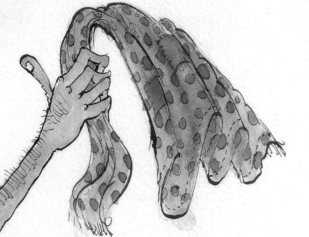

"Ready... steady...

START/FINISH

1st TURN

TO THE PALACE

N
W   E
S

Footpath

SHORT CUT

Strawberry Fields

SWAMP

Snail's House

POND

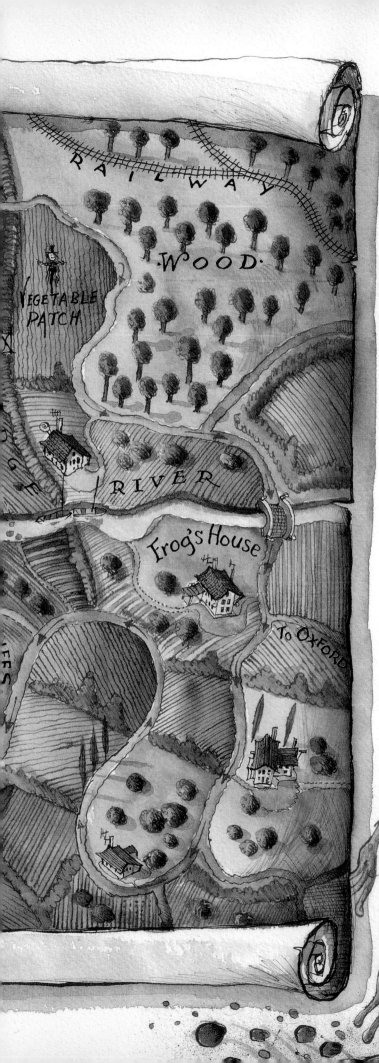

GO!"

The handkerchief dropped and the two friends started.

Frog bounded off at great speed but Snail was even faster. He moved so quickly that his feet polished the stones on the road as he passed over them.

Snail was over the bridge before Frog had even left the wood.

As Snail ran, he passed Frog's house and remembered
all the times the two of them had sat talking and laughing.

Snail stopped running and looked round.
He could see Frog coming down the path
from the wood.

He could see the determination on Frog's face.
Frog really did want to see the King.

Snail thought for a moment. He was only young. He had plenty of time to go and see the King. What had he been thinking, arguing with his old friend like that?

So Snail hid inside Frog's house and watched as his old friend staggered past. Frog was old and proud and Snail loved him. Frog deserved to see the King.

When Snail set off running again he went slowly, so he wouldn't catch up with Frog.

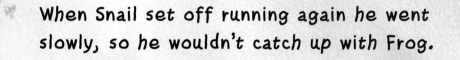

Frog had almost finished the race.
He could hardly believe it. He was going to win!
Frog could hear Snail close behind him...
but it was all over... he had won.

Frog had done it!

Snail crossed the finishing line and hugged his old friend.
"Well done! I didn't know you still had it in you!"

Frog gasped for breath and tried not to fall over.

"Well," said the chef. "It looks like Frog will be helping me with the King's birthday treat. You were very fast too," the chef told Snail. "I may come back for you another day."

The chef picked up Frog
and popped him into his
pocket, then headed off
back to the palace.

KYOHPA

PALACE

Frog went to the palace but
never actually saw the King.

But the King did agree that
the frog's legs were very good...
very good indeed.

When word got back to the wood about what
had happened to Frog, Snail was heartbroken.
He was also frightened that the chef
would come back for him!

So Snail took to wearing
his running hat on his
back and hiding
his legs inside it.

So if you ever see a snail in the daytime,
it will be crawling around on its tummy
with its legs hidden away just in case
a passing chef should ever remember
how good those legs really are.

But if you go outside early
in the morning you might just see
the tiny little trails that have been
left by some of the fastest snails
as their feet polish the floor
on their moonlight runs.

MORE TITLES FROM
FRANCES LINCOLN CHILDREN'S BOOKS

Best of Friends
Shen Roddie
Illustrated by Sally Anne Lambert

Hippo and Pig are neighbours as well as great friends.
Then one day, Hippo cuts down the hedge between them so
that they can see into each other's houses. Hippo is disgusted
on seeing his neighbour prancing around in a tutu, while Pig is
equally revolted by the sight of Hippo chewing his toenails.
Can they ever be friends again?

ISBN 978-1-84507-716-7

I Want a Pet
Lauren Child

I really want a pet: an African lion... or an octopus...
or even a boa constrictor... The trouble is, Mum and Dad and Granny
aren't keen on any of them. So I must try and find a pet that
none of them will mind. What could I have?

ISBN 978-0-71121-339-5

Ruby Sings the Blues
Niki Daly

Ruby's voice is so loud, it drives everyone crazy.
Her parents and teacher suggest that she turns down the volume,
but Ruby switches it up instead, and soon even her school friends
have had enough. Ruby feels blue, really blue – but Bernard and Zelda,
her jazz-playing neighbours have an idea...

ISBN 978-1-84507-280-3

Frances Lincoln titles are available from all good bookshops.
You can also buy books and find out more about your favourite titles,
authors and illustrators on our website: www.franceslincoln.com